FIREFIGHTER'S CURVY LITTLE

Age Play DDlg Romance

Amanda King

CONTENTS

CHAPTER 1

Lindsey

Eyes fluttering open, my pupils meeting the sunlight coming through the window. I yawned, the only thing I wanted to be doing right now being anything that wasn't me waking up. Sleeping was just so good. Sleeping in my bed was even better.

The mattress was so soft. I could spend hours – even more than that; days – hidden under the blankets.

So, so warm.

I looked outside and noticed that the color of the leaves was already changing. From green to yellow, orange, and even red.

Part of me just didn't want to get out of bed for all the possible reasons that existed. I felt like I was either on the moon or in heaven right now, my body floating.

But I still had to get out of bed, so that was what I did, pushing the blanket off my body. It fell on the floor, and then I dragged my legs over the mattress, letting my feet touch the floor. It touched the carpet, which was also as soft as the mattress, though also a little bit rougher.

I was naked. I lived alone and didn't have to worry about what other people might think about this. I just loved walking in my home naked, feeling the air against the skin of my body. There was something special about that. Something that I couldn't put into words. It felt… liberating.

I headed over to the window and looked outside again. Some trees dotted the garden behind my bedroom. It was located on the second floor, just above the living room. I lived in a two-story home and it had more rooms than I needed, but I would never trade it for another, smaller home.

I was doing pretty well for myself. I had more money than I needed and my career as a writer was gaining even more momentum than before. I had several books published under my pen name, and things were only going to keep getting better from now on.

I wanted to go outside now that I had already gotten out of bed. I wanted to play in the garden behind the bedroom. My eyes spotted some squirrels running behind the trees, and I wanted to go over there to play with them. I knew that they would run away, but I still wanted to do that.

My eyes checked the bedroom after turning around again. The walls were painted pink, a crib was positioned by one of the walls, there was a huge treasure chest with all my toys on the other side, and a childish, also pink, vanity by the main window, which I was going to use soon - right after I finished taking my wake-up shower, that was.

My ears could hear the birds chirping in the trees. Other than that, I couldn't hear anything. It was like, in this neighborhood, I was the only one that lived here. It was so serene, so peaceful. Thinking that, I just wanted to get behind my computer and start to write.

"It's going to be a very productive day, isn't it?" I happily said after grabbing my stuffed toy from the bed. I had to use most of my strength to grab it. It was as big as I was, fluffy, so soft, and also incredibly warm. I slept with it, just like I always did.

My eyes went to the right and I found this little pacifier I had to put into my mouth before going to bed last night. It was pink, just like everything in my bedroom. I loved the color so much. Even my stuffed toy had the same color. It was a pony and the color made it look even cuter than it was.

I put my stuffed pony back on the bed and went to the

bathroom. After taking a shower, I put on some clothes. Nothing extravagant this time, as usual. They were just some clothes to help me get through the day. Without them, I couldn't focus. I always got excited over what I was writing. I always imagined myself in the shoes of the main female character, and… Even more things than that happened. It was better not to even think about them. My body was already getting hot just remembering them.

After drying my hair and fixing my face after sitting down at the vanity, I headed to the other side of the bedroom, where my computer was. I turned it on and adjusted the firefighter chibi figure sitting by the side of the laptop.

If there was something I wanted, it was to have a firefighter for a boyfriend – or to be more specific about it, for a Daddy. Still, I knew that it would never happen. I wasn't going to get my hopes up about it. Why? It was pretty simple.

The more I thought about it, the more I realized that I didn't have many friends. This was my profession. It made me stay in my bedroom for hours on end, hoping that my words were going to please my readers, something that was getting harder by the day. As a writer, I always had to excel myself. It was a constant about me I doubted would ever change, I thought to myself after putting my fingers on the keyboard.

What was I going to write about today? I asked myself, typing away. As I typed on the keyboard, I decided I was going to write about a fraction of my life. I was going to write about a girl around my age who would, one day, find the love of her life.

And in the midst of all that, I was going to sprinkle some elements about age play and Daddy's Little Girl stuff, which I was certain my readers were going to love.

In the meantime, I was trying not to think about the party that I was going to have at my brother's place.

He was going to invite over many of his friends, including one of the firefighters in the city.

I didn't want to say this to myself again – I didn't even want to remember it – but there was no denying that I had a huge crush on him. It was so big I couldn't control it.

Especially when we were close and I could almost feel the warmth of his body.

CHAPTER 2

John

It was a party. I was at my friend's place. He was throwing this party where he decided to invite over everyone he knew. Really, pretty much everyone. The old woman across the street that always liked gossiping about his life, my ex-wife, my mom, and even his father, who was someone that he didn't like much at all.

He said that this party was supposed to amend all the bad things going on in his life. Maybe that was working, but... this still wasn't the kind of environment where I liked to find myself.

I wasn't trying to be grumpy, but the truth was that I didn't have many friends around here. I was in the middle of the party and trying to mingle, trying to talk to people, but more often than not I found myself lost.

The only thing I wanted to be doing right now was putting out fires. I was a firefighter, and it showed. It showed in the way that people looked at me. Whenever they looked at me, they always reminded themselves of the fact that I was a firefighter.

Either way, I wasn't going to let what was happening here make me feel even slightly depressed. So, without thinking anything about it, I decided to pad over to the other side of the living room. The party was happening at night and there weren't many people outside, so I couldn't just go there without everyone gossiping about me, saying that something was wrong with me.

Another thing that made me feel isolated here was that I was so much taller than everyone around here. Even though I couldn't know this for sure, I was certain that some people felt intimidated by that. Nothing I could do about it, though.

I turned around and started to make my way to that tiny spot across from where I was. It was a place where not many people were, so I could be there without feeling like there was an ocean of people surrounding me all the time. That thought alone was enough to make me feel so much more tempted.

I made my way there when I found someone crying. I blinked twice, trying to make myself think I was only imagining things. That had to be it, right? That was what I was telling myself anyway.

But it was more than obvious that I wasn't imagining anything. This party attendant was walking by me, and I stopped her so that I could put, on the platter that she was holding, the drink I had in my hand. I didn't want to drink anything anymore. I wasn't much of a drinker, anyway.

Actually, my mind was focused on something else. My mind was focused on the woman sitting outside the house. She wasn't just crying; she had her face buried in her hands.

She looked nothing short of beautiful and, even if she weren't crying, I would be talking to her right at this moment. Still, I was doing this because I was someone with a good heart. At least, that was what my mom always told me before she passed away last year. My heart still felt the impact of that night.

Not to mention that I was a firefighter. Helping people was something I always did, even when it didn't involve me putting out fires.

I opened the door and found myself outside the house and with her. She was crying and sobbing so loudly she didn't hear me coming over. She was noticeably younger than me and had coconut hair and fair skin.

I would never say this to her – unless we were in the right moment and under the appropriate circumstances – but I was already developing a small crush on her. Knowing that it would most likely never amount to anything, I kept my lips sealed. I wouldn't want her to think that I was here just to hit on her.

I sat down. She was sitting down on the porch steps that faced the backyard.

This place was serene. I could see the moon in the sky and even though I could still hear the music and people chatting and laughing inside the house, it was all nothing more than background noise to me.

I waited to see if she was going to notice my presence. After all, I was a big man. Not to mention that, before coming over to this party, I had also sprayed perfume on me. I wasn't one to wear perfume, but for tonight I thought it was going to do something different. Perhaps I was finally going to find someone interested in me.

I mean, someone interested in me as something more than how much she could use me before dumping me. I didn't like to think about it this way, but most women in the city only wanted me for sex.

I didn't work out, but I kept myself in shape. I supposed that it was all thanks to my job. It was not easy to work as a firefighter. It was hard, stressful, and more often than not I found myself in situations where I could die.

Still, I wasn't thinking about that at the moment. I was a Daddy. Always had been since turning 25 and I realized that most relationships weren't for me. That was when I had my first Little, but she also wasn't the one for me.

I mean, we had even gotten married and she was great in the first months, but then things started to deteriorate. Small things started to annoy me and I soon found myself fed up with her. That was one of the reasons why I ended up leaving. I was the one that made the difficult choice in the end, I reaffirmed.

Then, the woman by my side finally lifted her head from her hands. She looked at me, her eyes red and hurt. Now, more than ever before, I was beginning to think I found someone else I wanted to protect – more so than every time I put on my firefighter uniform.

This woman was... someone that could stoke something different in my heart. Something that I'd forgotten about a long time ago.

CHAPTER 3

So, that was why I was here. This party didn't have much to do with me. And now here I was. I was with this man sitting by my side. He had a concerned, friendly look in his eyes. Something that I couldn't quite put my finger on, but which was drawing me to him the more time passed. I was certain he was thinking something was wrong with me.

After all, I was staring at him and doing nothing else, this feeling creepier by the second. I shouldn't be doing this.

"I'm sorry, have we met before?" I asked. He cleared his throat, showing me that he was caught off guard by my question.

"No, I don't think we have. I was just walking behind the door when I noticed you crying. I just thought that I should come over and check up on you."

Check up on me? I asked myself, suddenly realizing that there was someone at this party that actually cared about me. And he was a total stranger, too. I couldn't believe what my eyes were witnessing and what my ears were hearing.

Not even my brother, who invited me to this party, had shown any interest in what was going on in my mind. And I'd thought that we were close, that he was going to shoot me question after question, asking me about my stories.

After all, when I had told him before that I was a writer,

he seemed interested in the subject. But now, looking over my shoulder, all I could see was that he was with his wife, laughing and chatting with his friends loudly. I could hear everything they were saying even though I was outside and the sound was muffled.

"I'm sorry. I didn't want anyone to worry about me," I said.

"You don't need to be sorry about something like that. It's okay to cry, especially when something is troubling you." There was a moment of silence and he didn't say anything, making me wonder what he was thinking right now. "Though, I suppose I should first introduce myself. I'm John."

And I supposed that now I should be saying that I actually knew him, I thought now that he said his name. I had thought that we had met before, but we really hadn't. He was a firefighter. He was from the local department.

Now that he said his name, I remembered him. He was John. My brother's best friend. He lived alone in his house, always making me wonder how someone of his caliber had not found someone he wanted to marry yet.

So many of my supposed friends always had so many good things to tell me about him. They always told me that he was a charmer, that he cared about people thanks to his firefighter background, that he bought gifts for everyone he liked, showed them that they were really important to him, and there were so many other things he did that I felt overwhelmed thinking about them.

Also, his looks. He was, without a shred of doubt, stunning. He was mouthwatering. Even now, even though his eyes were examining me closely, I felt saliva building up in my mouth, and I couldn't do anything about that. It was just happening. I was certain that John was soon going to notice that. The first thing he would do after his mind was aware of this little reaction my body was experiencing, would be to run away from me.

I hoped that he wouldn't do that, but... Worse things had already happened before in my life.

"I'm Lindsey," I said, hoping that I wasn't sounding like a total fool, but knowing full well that I still did.

"Do you… want to tell me why you were crying?"

I should. I should do that, but the truth was that I couldn't. I couldn't because I knew what he would say. He would start to ask me more and more questions about why this was happening, and after everything going on here, I just didn't want to talk to anyone about anything.

When I came to this party, the first thought that crossed my mind was that I would never have what these people had. I would never find love. Nobody would ever want me like that, and… I'd gotten desperate. That was the first thought that crossed my mind, now that I was thinking about this in more detail.

"No. It's nothing against you, but I don't think I should tell anyone about what's going on in my life," I said, standing up. I stood up in a heartbeat when my eyes caught sight of something rather scary happening close by.

A shadow ran in the dark among the trees that surrounded this house. I hoped that I was just imagining things, but then I realized that wasn't the case. Or was it? The more I thought about this, the more I wanted to think this was all nothing more than just my mind playing tricks on me.

My right foot slipped and I soon found myself falling over the porch steps. I thought I was going to hit my head on the ground when I found his arms going around me. His arms were strong and muscular. I felt safe in them, which was something that I had not felt in a very long time.

"Woah, I think that you need to be a little more careful when standing up." And I hoped that he was going to add, right at the end, 'Little One.' But he didn't. He did appear to have all the right attributes to be a Daddy, but no way he was, I thought. I was pretty much alone in this town.

I had money, but I didn't have someone that made my life feel complete, and that was something that would never change.

"Uhh, thanks," I said when he took his arms off me, making me realize that I wanted his arms around me all the time. What I would not do to feel his arms around me one more time, keeping me safe, especially when I was going to fall over. And now that I was thinking about it, that was something that was beginning to happen more often.

I looked into his eyes and said, "I think I should go now, but… thanks for checking up on me anyway and looking like the only one here that cares about me."

So that was my introduction to John and it was awkward. At least he helped to make me feel better, but we didn't talk much and I didn't tell him anything about my life, or why I was crying. I shouldn't, anyway. So, that was something I avoided and I was thankful for it, but still…

I still couldn't help but wonder what he thought about me now that he noticed me at that party.

He *noticed* me. It had to mean something, right?

CHAPTER 4

John

What, you thought that something was really going to happen between you two? I asked myself, looking at the ceiling. I was alone in my house. I was looking at the ceiling. It was dark outside and the only thing I wanted to do right now was to feel her in my arms once again. But I was certain that it would never happen.

I still couldn't stop scrutinizing and dwelling on the fact that she left me just like that.

I looked at the side and found a portrait sitting on top of the nightstand. It was a portrait of me and my wife. *My ex-wife*, I corrected myself.

I sat up on the bed, rubbing my eyes with my hands.

Nothing was going to make me get over what happened between us. She was audacious enough to cheat on me, and that was something I would never get over. She cheated on me with someone else here in the city. At least they had the decency of moving out of here. Where were they living today? I didn't know, but either way, it didn't matter.

What mattered was that I was here and there was finally someone in the city that caught my attention. She was my best friend's sister and was stunning. One of the most beautiful, memorable people I had seen in my life.

And in my line of work, I had seen so many people, so that was saying something.

I put the portrait down. Seeing my wife and remembering that life we had together wasn't going to help me with anything. If anything, it was only making me feel more depressed than I already was.

That was what I was telling myself over and over anyway, hoping that my shitty brain was finally going to accept that, but time passed and nothing changed.

I just couldn't stop thinking about this one thing – I was already over 35 years old and still single. Every time that I went online, when I logged into Instagram, I saw my friends and family having the time of their lives, married and with children.

I didn't know anything about having children, but I still wanted someone that wanted to live with me for the rest of her life.

I groaned when I found myself in the bathroom, planting my hands on the sink. I stared at myself in the mirror and decided to start to think about something I would rather not do. I should not do this, whatever it was that was beginning to spring out in my mind.

It wasn't going to help me or anyone. And yet… I still wanted to get to know her better.

Lindsey.

So, I just grabbed my phone and looked her up. I knew that she had to be on one of the more typical social media websites. Facebook, Instagram, TikTok, and plenty of others, and I was hoping that I was going to find her. I wanted to chat with her.

I wanted to find out if Lindsey thought the same way about me – or, at least, to get to know her better. Now that I was thinking better about this, it was becoming so obvious that she was my new obsession.

I hated it every time that it happened. I hated it whenever I had an obsession with someone.

So, I typed her first name and then her last one. I knew her last name thanks to the fact that she was my best friend's sister. It shouldn't be too difficult to find her, I thought after scrolling down the page and then doing the same with another page, hoping that I was going to find that face I knew so well.

I started to pace back and forth in the bathroom, hoping that I was going to find her profile. When I finally did, I wouldn't hesitate. I would add her and then I would see what would happen from then on.

Minutes later, I was about to give up, groaning, feeling some sweat breaking out on my forehead when I finally found her profile picture on the left side of the screen.

That was her.

And the best thing about this? It was that she had not hidden her photos from anyone to see. I could see all of them without having to add her, and that was really great. My heart started to beat a little faster than normal, but I didn't think much of it. Yet.

What I was thinking about at the moment was how I was going to approach this.

CHAPTER 5

Lindsey

I was eating cereal from the bowl on the table in the kitchen when I heard the ping coming from my phone. For a moment, I didn't think much of it, but then I decided to check it. I just wanted to make sure that it wasn't anything important. Chances were that it was just someone that wanted to strike a financial deal with me, perhaps to help me with promoting my books.

But then, I noticed that the notification actually came from someone else. It came from a man. And after checking out his profile picture, I almost spat out the cereal I was munching. It was John. He was the firefighter that was so worried about me when he met me at that party.

This was the day after that, so I was still thinking about him. I never thought that he would just find me on Facebook.

My finger hovered over the accept button. I knew I shouldn't, but something in me told me that he wanted to talk to me. This was no accident. This was not Facebook being creepy – again – and connecting me with someone I had met at the party.

No, this was him looking me up and finding me out of his own accord.

I still pressed the accept button and then I noticed that my heart was speeding up. Minutes passed and he didn't send me any message. He should have looked me up because he wanted to talk to me, right?

I dropped my phone on the table, suddenly finding myself annoyed with myself and with him. Why the hell did he add me on Facebook if he didn't want to chat with me right away? I asked myself.

Just when I was going to give up and was going to bed, another notification popped up on the screen. This time, I turned on the screen in a heartbeat and checked where the notification came from.

It came from John.

John: Hey, I know that this is sudden, but I just wanted to make sure that you are feeling okay. I'm John, from your brother's party.

My heart was tight. I knew that this was about much more than just his concern for me, I thought.

Me: I'm okay, really. I remember you from the party.

John: Do you want to talk about what was happening? I know that I don't have any right to know anything, but I'm still worried. Perhaps that's one of my biggest faults. I'm always worried about everyone that could use my help.

This was awkward, but now that it already started, there was no point in going back.

How was I going to explain to him why I was crying? If I said anything about it, he would just laugh at me, call me a loser, and maybe do something even worse than that. That was why I wasn't exactly thrilled about this chat we were having.

I decided to go to the bedroom. This was where I felt much more comfortable, especially now that I was feeling so much anxiety.

I lied down on the bed, already feeling much more relieved. I felt like I had control over this chat we were having.

But now that I was thinking about this again and much more profoundly than before, I felt rage bubbling up in my veins. This would not be the first time a man was getting obsessed with me for no apparent reason.

After all, even though John was a firefighter, my crush, so hot, and so much everything else, this was still... I didn't even want to use the word I was conjuring up in my mind.

I wasn't going to and I was going to end this conversation right now.

Me: I'm sorry, but I don't know why you added me, but this chat really can't go anywhere. I can't tell you anything about what's going on in my life.

John: But you are my Wesley's sister. If you don't want to tell him anything about what's going on in your life, then you can talk to me. I'm just saying that you don't need to be alone.

I shook my head, turning off the chat window and then blocking him. After I did that, the first thing that crossed my mind was that I was going to regret it.

After all, I didn't even give myself the chance to check his profile. I was sure that someone like him, who was so much more like a man of the mountains, didn't have much information on his Facebook account.

At least, that was what I told myself.

I dropped my phone on the floor. Then, I ran my hands over my face, hating myself for this. I had thought that this was a good chance to get to know him more personally, but it wasn't going to happen anymore.

It wasn't going to happen because no matter what came to pass from now on, I wasn't going to unblock him on Facebook.

I had so many things about my life sorted out, but when it came to my love life, I felt so lost.

That was why I wasn't going to do this. I was going to the bathroom, take a shower, and then I was going to play with my toys on the floor. Then, tonight, I was going to sleep in the crib, and it was going to be great and I was going to feel like I would never even have to see John again.

Given the fact that I could work at home without ever having to worry about going out — even my grocery I always bought online — I was certain I would never have any reason to meet up with him in person.

At least, that was what I was telling myself so that I could sleep better tonight.

CHAPTER 6

John

Just when I was going to close my eyes, I heard her message on the phone. What the hell? I asked myself. I thought that she had already blocked me. At least, that was what it looked like to me when I read her last message. I thought she was fed up with me. I should have realized that texting her in the middle of the night was a bad idea.

Lindsey: I was crying because I can't find anyone.

She couldn't find anyone? I asked myself, for the first few seconds trying to rationalize this. She couldn't find anyone as in 'she was single and feeling lonely?'

I didn't want to think this was the case, but if that was what was going on here, then I couldn't help but wonder if it was the opportunity I was looking for. If she was, perhaps, the person that could make my life whole.

But I wasn't going to get ahead of myself. She wanted to talk to me now and that was great.

Me: what do you mean that you can't find anyone?

Lindsey: I mean that I'm alone. I spend most of my days writing, trying to please my readers, and always alone in my house. It's a big house. It's great. It has everything I could ever need, but it's still not enough when I don't have anyone to chat with a little about my problems. Not to mention that I broke up with the only person I thought was the right one for me, but that was such a long time ago… and I should be over it already… The more I think about this, the more pathetic I feel.

Me: you don't need to feel pathetic about wanting to make your life feel better. I'm single too, in case you are wondering. I don't have anyone. I don't have any family here. Most of my nights, I'm all by myself. I think about it all the time, so I can definitely relate to what you are saying.

And then, nothingness. I wondered what Lindsey was thinking right now. Three dots appeared on the screen and I thought she was finally going to reply back, but then nothing happened. To be honest, after everything going on here, I just wanted to make sure she was okay.

Or was going to be okay.

In the meantime, I couldn't help but wonder what it would be like to find another Little in my life. But I didn't think that such a thing would ever happen here in this town. It was too small, after all.

I knew about the existence of two other Littles here, not lying to myself. But they were both taken already. Gloria and Jackie… We didn't talk often, but I knew they were doing well. They didn't talk much about their lives and certainly didn't feel like finding out if other people were in the lifestyle, too.

We met up so little that, more often than not, it did really feel like I was the only one in town in the lifestyle. The only Daddy. The only one who knew about age play and ABDL stuff…

Lindsey: I didn't know anything about that. I thought that you had a girlfriend. I mean, everyone I know that knows about you always says you are a good person, that you could be a great husband, and I'm certain that they are right about all that.

I chuckled. People were saying those things about me? I didn't know anything about that.

And while I continued texting her after finding out that she unblocked me, I also resumed checking her photos on Facebook, finding out that most of them involved her and her book promos. It looked like she was having an amazing time writing her stories,

I thought.

She did have family here, but given what the photos showed me, it looked like they weren't close. Not close like I'd been with my family. Now all I had was my friend and some of the guys I knew from the fire station.

Me: There are so many things about me you don't know.

And then, nothingness again. I was lying on my bed, my other hand going to my cock. I started to stroke it gently, imagining that Lindsey was my Little and that she was with me on my bed, lowering her head and wrapping her lips around my dickhead. If that ever happened, I would be so happy.

But I had again to tell myself it would never happen. The only thing that Lindsey and I had in common was that we were both feeling lonely.

Lindsey: I don't know if I should do this…

Me: do what?

Lindsey: Do you wanna… come over? I can give you my address. I think I would like to have you over. Just give me some time and don't come here too quickly. I need to get some things ready.

I wondered what she meant by 'getting some things ready,' but I quickly pushed that thought out of my mind. It wasn't going to help me right now with anything.

Linsey was inviting me over to her house, and I could not say no. So, this was a date? It sure looked like it was.

Me: why didn't you say it before? I'm definitely going.

Lindsey: thanks. I knew you were going to say that.

I threw my phone over the bed, sat up on it, and then got myself ready for the date. It had been such a long time since my last date that I couldn't believe this was happening like this.

I didn't want to feel like I was a teenager all over again, but that was exactly what was happening right now.

Still, I had to keep my hopes about this quenched. I just didn't want to think that we would ever be in a serious relationship. After all, there was just no chance it would ever happen. When it came down to it, I was a Daddy and she was just a person, an author of books, and she had a big house and a lot more money than I could ever imagine I would have, one day, in my life.

At least, that was what I was telling myself, though part of me still thought this was the beginning of something much bigger than that.

In less than a few seconds, I was ready. I put on some nice clothes, sprayed perfume again, checked myself out in the mirror one more time, and then brushed the lock of my hair that refused to stay in place and kept falling in front of my right eye.

How annoying.

Still, it was such a tiny little thing in the face of this date I was going to have with Lindsey.

CHAPTER 7

So, this was really happening and I felt more nervous about this than ever before in my life. That was why it took me so long to hide everything that was in my bedroom. I knew that this was going to be a date. It was going to be my first time with a man. Not my first time having sex, but my first time doing it with a man.

I was bisexual, so I had some experiences with my former girlfriend.

This should mean that it's done, right? I asked, my eyes scanning the bedroom one more time. I was in front of the doorway, realizing that I still needed to touch up my makeup a little.

I wasn't one to wear makeup, so this was all unfamiliar territory to me.

After some minutes, I realized that nothing was wrong with my bedroom. When he came here, he would think that I was a woman like everyone else. He would not think that something else was at play here.

I had to hide pretty much everything that related to me being a Little. My stuffed pony, my crib, and even my toy chest, I thought while feeling some tightness in my heart.

I hated that I had to hide so much of my life so that my date didn't go haywire from the start.

But such was life and I couldn't do anything about it.

After ascertaining that everything in my bedroom was where it was supposed to be, I rushed over into the bathroom, throwing open the door and then opening my makeup box one more time. Everything I needed to use was here.

So, I used lipstick, blush, eyeliner, and pretty much everything else so that my face looked exactly how I wanted it to look. Even after I put everything back inside the box, I still had to check myself out in the mirror one more time to make sure that nothing was wrong.

And truly, nothing was.

I took a deep breath in when I headed back into my bedroom, and it was then I heard the doorbell ring. Oh shit, I thought to myself after realizing that this was really going to happen. In the beginning, it had felt like I was maybe just trying to rationalize this, but now it was so much more obvious that it was happening and there was nothing about it I could do.

I rushed over to the door and opened it, my heart speeding up. Even breathing was becoming difficult. I blinked twice. The man that was standing in front of me was still... The same man from before. He didn't change at all.

I thought that he was going to put on a suit, a tie, nice leather boots, and that he was going to make his face glow with something that only men could use but which wouldn't be awkward at all, but that wasn't what I was seeing at all.

It was much different from that. The man standing in front of me was still John, and he was just John. John the firefighter. John, the man willing to put his life on the line to keep everyone protected. John, the man that didn't stop himself before putting his arms around me that night, impeding me from falling.

He was breathtaking and even though I should be saying something and inviting him inside my house, I couldn't.

His stare had me locked in place, and I didn't know what I was supposed to be doing.

After a while, he cleared his throat, putting his hands in his pockets. I didn't know why this was happening – or maybe I did and I just didn't want to admit it – but my eyes couldn't stop examining every little movement that he did.

"Can I come in?" He asked and his voice was, again, like music to my ears. That time when we talked at Wesley's house, I didn't have much time or was in the right state of mind to appreciate it, but now that I could, it was so much more than I thought it was going to be.

"Sure, yeah," I finally said after trying to make myself look less like the fool and the dumb girl in class that I now looked like.

I stepped to the side, letting him in. He walked into my house showing respect in his eyes, though it was obvious that he was still studying everything that he could. Every tiny little bit about this that he could see with his eyes, he was checking it all, from left to right, and it made me feel more nervous than I already was.

It made me feel more like that because I knew what was happening here. After my breakup with my girlfriend, I didn't know if I could ever feel love again. But… this was exactly what was happening here, wasn't it? This wasn't exactly love yet, but it was beginning to feel more and more like it.

"It's a nice house. You surely have a lot of money," he said and now that I could see his back, I felt like I could think better about what was happening here. John really wore nothing much different from when he was at Wesley's party. Nothing at all. Just a white shirt, jeans, and black shoes, and that was pretty much it.

And I supposed that, now, I'd better invite him to have dinner with me.

CHAPTER 8

John

But we didn't have dinner. We were just drinking. Still, just drinking and doing not much more than that, other than chatting a little. She was with me in the kitchen. When I first entered it, I couldn't stop my eyes from turning left and right, checking everything. Her kitchen... I could imagine myself cooking here, cooking something for her, though I imagined that something like that would never happen.

At least, that was what I was telling myself.

Lindsey was so pretty, even now that she looked a little drunk. Her cheeks were blushing slightly. She had her glass in her hand and was turning it slowly, the liquid sloshing about shyly.

"So many things happened in my life before this," she confessed, not looking anywhere in particular. She was telling me about her life. She was telling me about her breakup with her girlfriend.

She had gone through so much, making me want to do just one thing – to wrap her in my arms and tell her that everything was going to be fine.

"Do you want to tell me how it all went down? Then, maybe I can tell you something about what happened in my relationship as well."

"There was this one day when I already had a terrible,

uncontrollable feeling in me. It was like a premonition. I was already thinking that it was all going to be ruined that day."

And right after she said that, she shed a tear and it rolled down her cheek. All right, enough waiting was enough, I thought, putting my drink down on the kitchen island and then easing my arm around her. She needed support and I was going to give it to her right at this moment.

Lindsey looked at me, her lips parting slowly. I didn't think that she was going to make a fuss about this and she didn't, which made me feel more certain about her feelings for me.

She looked into my eyes, examining them. I wondered exactly what she was thinking, and I didn't have to be wondering about it for much longer.

"It was on that day when I found out she was going through all my messages on Instagram. She was going behind my back to find out about everything I was talking about with my friends and work colleagues. We had an argument, I started to yell so many terrible things at her, and then she just up and left, leaving me alone in my house. It all happened right in this spot where we are standing right now."

I looked down, imagining this happening, Lindsey being angry, shouting, saying all kinds of obscenities, and for some reason, it all felt so surreal. I just couldn't imagine her being anything different from the usual, sweet self she was.

"I'm really sorry about all that."

She finished her drink, setting the glass down on the kitchen island. "And, now do you want to tell me a little about what happened when you were still with your wife?"

I knew that she would eventually ask me that question, but I was still hoping that she wasn't going to. Now that I was thinking better about this, it hurt me so much to remember all the events that transpired that day.

But I still didn't move away from her. Doing that would have been rude and I didn't want Lindsey to think that way about me.

I sighed and felt her hand settling on top of mine, showing me her support. I knew that she was going to give me support now that I was going through all the events that happened on that infamous day.

"She was cheating on me with someone else. I mean, I had gotten suspicious when I noticed that she was chatting on the phone at night when she thought I was sleeping, but then I ended up finding out the truth when I followed her one day and she was with this guy. I couldn't believe what my eyes were seeing. I just couldn't. I confronted her then and there, and I told her how I felt about it. I told her that I didn't want anything to do with her anymore."

After saying that, I noticed that my voice was changing. It was becoming throatier, huskier, and it was the first time I noticed it changing so much thanks to my break up with my wife.

"I'm so sorry about that. We should never hide secrets from the people we care about, and the moment when we stop caring about someone, I think... it's the moment when we should put it all behind us and look forward to something else."

I looked down, finding her sparkling eyes. Her lips - I couldn't stop looking at them and now, more than ever before, I just wanted to kiss her. The only problem with that was that I couldn't do it without it feeling awkward and catching her off guard, though now that I was thinking about this, I supposed that Lindsey was... kind of expecting it? I didn't know, but my body was begging for it.

"It's okay. She left and then I decided to start my life anew. That was the reason why I decided to switch jobs and I found myself here in Sudbury. Now you know everything about me."

Or almost everything. She would never find out about the fact I was a Daddy.

And now, Lindsey was just looking at me without saying anything. I didn't want to think that this was really happening, but I felt like there was a force pulling my head down and I couldn't stop it. In less than a few seconds, when I thought that I was just dreaming this, she kissed me.

She kissed me and it was the most memorable, most frightening, and also most sweet kiss I had had in a very long time in my life. After all, this whole time, I had never kissed anyone after my wife moved away from me.

CHAPTER 9

What? I asked myself, trying to understand what was happening here. We were still kissing. I had not told him anything about my Little side, though now that this was happening, I was beginning to think that I should, even if only to make sure that nothing else would ever come out of this. I just didn't want him to think that we could be more than this. We would never be boyfriend and girlfriend because that wasn't the only thing I was looking for. I was looking for a Daddy.

John pulled his head back, resting his hand on my cheek.

"Lindsey..."

"Don't say anything. Just kiss me again," I affirmed after planting my hands on his cheeks, pulling his head down for another hot kiss. I felt his lips pressing against mine, his tongue coming inside my mouth, and I moaned, his hands roaming over the sides of my body, feeling me.

He loved what he was feeling and I felt myself getting overwhelmed by his immense presence, his body engulfing mine.

"I'm not stopping this, no matter what you say," he affirmed right into my mouth as he continued kissing me, one sizzling hot peck after the other, making me feel more overwhelmed than I already felt.

"I'm not asking you to stop," I murmured when I felt his hands pulling up my shirt. I was just letting it all happen. John finished pulling up my shirt, revealing for the delight of his eyes my exposed chest. He took in what his eyes were seeing, breathing out loudly.

"You are so stunning, Lindsey."

I had thought that he would never say something like that. I was… a little on the curvy side, always thinking that I should lose some weight, but now that he was complimenting me on how my body looked, I had fewer reasons to think that I should change anything about it.

I thought that there was nothing that could make me feel much better than how I already felt.

We stopped and for a moment it was like neither of us knew what to do. But then, he pulled me until I was sitting on the kitchen island, his hands grabbing my thighs. I could feel John's fingers digging into the skin.

I didn't know what to say, especially when his fingers started to remove my pants. I didn't have much say in what was happening here. I could feel his fingers dragging across my thighs, sending electrical shocks in my body.

My pussy was already wet and I didn't know how much wetter it could get.

As if this wasn't enough, John started to rub and draw circles on my clit, stimulating the overwhelming pleasure that was already seeping out of my body. I started to moan and groan, his finger picking up the pace before slowing down.

I kicked my panties away from me. Then, without giving me as much as a warning, John started to take off his clothes. He was fast doing it. One piece at a time, he peeled off all of his clothes, showing me his perfect body. It made my mouth water just thinking about how I was going to feel when I had my hands traveling over his muscles, feeling the lines and how defined they were.

I just couldn't believe that this was happening. The firefighter, the one who was my crush, was about to fuck me.

"Gosh, you are irresistible," he murmured into my ear, leaning over and then rubbing his body against mine. The way he did that made me feel like I was going to pass out. His body was so big that it blocked most of the light in front of my eyes.

I couldn't say anything. My lips were sealed.

Then, John swept me up in his arms, making me gasp. "What are you doing?" I asked as I raised my voice. I just wanted to know where he was taking me.

"I'm taking you somewhere better, where we can truly do this without anything getting in the way and I can feel how much this truly means to me."

I didn't know what to say. One moment he was walking with me in his arms to my bedroom, and then the next he kicked the door open, leading me into my bedroom. A moment later, John laid me down on the bed.

When I blinked, he was on top of me, his arms on both sides of my body. I had just about enough time to gasp when he came crashing down, his lips pressing against mine while his hand looked for the only thing that he wanted the most, which was my hot, quivering pussy.

I had just about enough time, again, when he showed me that he had a condom in his hand. I didn't even realize that he had it with him. I thought that he had left his pants on the floor in the kitchen.

I supposed that this was happening because my mind was such a whirlwind of different thoughts right now.

I should be paying more attention to what was happening, I thought when he penetrated me and then went all the way inside to the hilt. I couldn't see his cock. He was so deep inside of me that he hurt me. It was the first time that a man was inside of me and it was an experience like no other.

"Oh fuck, oh fuck," I said over and over, trying to continue to breathe while he fucked me over and over, his balls slapping against my ass, pushing me over the edge when he climaxed at the same time as I did.

It was truly an experience I would never have again.

CHAPTER 10

Lindsey

It was the next morning, the sunlight shining through the window. I opened my eyes and expected to see him by my side in the bed, but my hand found nothing. I had no idea where he was, but my fingers were still looking, still pressing into the bedsheets, and my nose was still searching for the odor of his body. I knew that it was somewhere in the air.

And yet, I just couldn't. I couldn't find anything. I couldn't find his presence in the bed, in the air, or in any place in my room. Even though I didn't want to think that this was exactly what was happening, I was already making the assumption that he'd left me. Especially after finding out that there was something wrong with me – something he should know about – and something that I should've said to him when he was here.

But then, my nose picked up a certain smell in the air. I didn't want to think that it might be what I was hoping it was, but that wasn't how my mind worked. My mind was already starting to think that it was the smell of someone cooking something in the kitchen. Whoever that was, I was soon going to find out, especially because I lived alone in my house and I wasn't going crazy, suddenly finding out that someone had moved in.

So, I stood up and put on whatever clothes I could. I hoped that I was going to find out that he was still here and in the kitchen, but again, I wasn't going to get my hopes up - not any more than they already were. After the disappointment I had with my girlfriend, I didn't want to be disappointed with anyone, and that was something I was promising myself right at this moment – one more time.

So, I went to the kitchen and found him. John. He was in front of the stove, moving his arms and hands, working on cooking something. Oh, the smell. It was absolutely delicious. I just couldn't believe that John himself was cooking something for me. He was making my brunch, and the smell coming from the stove was enough to suggest to me that he was adding bacon strips too, which were necessary for every brunch I had.

He turned around, smiling. "I'm sorry. I didn't think that you were just going to show up all of a sudden while I'm still cooking. I thought I was going to have more time." John chuckled. "And you don't need to worry. After I'm done here, I'll leave. I just don't want anyone to think that I'm here to stay."

"No, you can stay. I didn't think that you were actually going to start to cook for me. I thought that you were going to leave as soon as you said goodbye to me."

"I could never do that. I'm just happy that we shared so much about ourselves with each other," he said and then I sat down on the chair, waiting for him to finish cooking the brunch. And he did that some minutes later, and he was a lot faster about it than I would have been if it were me doing the cooking.

I dug in right away, feeling how tasty the food was. It was delicious. I started to eat everything and I wasn't going to stop – not until nothing was left. Even John was surprised by what his eyes were witnessing. He didn't think that I was going to like his food so much.

"Well, I'm happy that you are enjoying the food so much," he said and he ate with me. After that, we kissed one more time. How many times could we still kiss each other? I didn't know, but I supposed that it was so many more times it was pointless to count. After doing that, John even did the dishes, something I didn't expect from him. Now that I was thinking better about this, he was showing me more and more that he had all the right attributes to be a Daddy.

Again, I wasn't going to get my hopes up. It was good enough that we were already sharing this moment after he finished doing the dishes.

After John finished that, he came with me back into my bedroom. I had everything I had related to my Little side locked in one of the closets. It was where I was keeping everything that John shouldn't see.

He pushed me against the closet door, and I gasped. I looked up and found his intense eyes staring right back into mine. I wanted to kiss his lips. I wanted to do that again.

But I was also not in my right state of mind. If I were, I would have pushed him away from me right at this moment.

I could feel the door behind me giving in. We were both going to fall into the closet and I couldn't do anything about this. It was already too late, anyway, I thought when I felt him throwing his arms around me one more time. It was just like that time when we were at Wesley's.

Except that, this time, he could see everything. Everything that I was hiding. My toy chest, the crib, the stuffed pony, my coloring books, and pretty much everything that pertained to my Little side.

The next thing I did was look into his eyes. They were wide eyes. He showed me that he didn't think he was going to find something so childish in my closet. But it wasn't just one thing, of course. There were many childish things that he couldn't wrap his head around – not without thinking that there was something deeply wrong with me.

"Wait, are you really telling me that you are a Little?" He asked, making me blush. For a moment, I couldn't understand what he'd just said. I thought that John was going to dump me. I thought that he was going to accuse me of being a pedophile, but that wasn't what he was suggesting.

Perhaps I was really looking into the person that could become my Daddy.

CHAPTER 11

"Wait, are you really telling me what I'm thinking you are telling me?" I asked, hoping that I wasn't imagining things. John was telling me that he knew about Littles and Daddies? This felt so surreal, to put it mildly.

"Yeah, I do know about this. I'm not sure if I should be so blunt about it, but I'm a Daddy. I've always been ever since I found out that it is everything I've always wanted to be."

I blinked twice, not really understanding what he was saying, but still just knowing that it was good. It was so good that I couldn't contain myself when it happened. I threw my arms around him, burying my head in his chest. It was kind of crazy what was happening, but I was welcoming it nonetheless.

"You are a Daddy?" I asked, rubbing my head on his chest. I didn't even know why I was doing it. I felt like I was doing everything in my power so that I felt as much of his body as I could. "It's so good to know."

It made me feel like everything I went through in my life didn't mean anything. It made me feel like I just wanted him to diaper me and put me to sleep in my crib. I was sure he was thinking the same thing. I was sure that our date was going to kickstart our relationship, too.

"Yeah. As I said, I'm a Daddy. So, this means you are a Little, right?" He asked, moving his hand around the back of my head. He was caressing it. I looked up and found his comforting, warm eyes.

"Yeah, I am. You know that I was thinking all this time you might be a Daddy, but I was so afraid to ask anything about it because, if you didn't know anything about this, I thought that you were going to say it was creepy."

He smiled. "That was exactly why I was afraid of ever bringing this up. I was thinking that you might stop talking to me and never even want to see me again because of it."

"I was really thinking the same thing, too," I said when I realized that he was looking over my shoulder and at something behind me. I didn't know what that was, so I turned around and I immediately found out what had caught his attention so much.

It was my crib. He was looking at it and I was certain he wanted to ask me something about it.

"So, this is your crib and your other things. You put all of this in the closet so that I didn't see anything when I was here."

I smiled. Of course that was the reason why I did it. But now that he was saying that out loud, I felt so much more nervous about it. I felt like I was overreacting. I just never thought that John was so open-minded.

"Yeah, that was why I did it. My thought process was that I had my date with you and I didn't want to ruin it because of anything."

He rubbed my head. His skin was warm and I felt goosebumps all through my body.

"Now that you know I'm a Daddy, you don't need to hide anything from me anymore, even though nothing of this means that we should be in a relationship or anything of the sort. I just don't want to make you think that I'm forcing this on you or anything like that. Knowing that we are both in the same lifestyle doesn't mean that we should be together."

I felt my cheeks blushing. I knew that this was taking a huge step, but it still felt like the right one. John took my hand in his, showing me that, no matter what happened now, he had my back, and that was a lot more than I thought I would ever have.

"But I want to be with you. I want to be your Little. After

getting to know you and after spending some time with you, I just want you to know that I... love you. I know that I probably shouldn't be saying this to someone I haven't been with long yet, but... yeah. This is still happening," I confessed.

And then, John kissed me one more time, his hand going down my body and cupping my right asscheek.

"I think that someone in here probably needs something a little different, something that is going to make her day feel even better than this," he murmured into my mouth and then kissed me again and then so many more times I lost count. I didn't want to say this, but I was gasping for air. The many times that he kissed me were enough to remove all the air that was in my lungs.

"Do you want to change my diaper? Or I mean that do you want to put my diaper on me?" I asked, moving my hand over his shoulder and feeling how hard his muscles were.

"Do I want to do that?" He chuckled, kissing me one more time and, this time, it was on my right cheek. "I think that I want to do so much more than that. I want to be with you all the time. You don't mind if I move in, right?" He asked, making me feel tingles of excitement over my skin.

My Daddy coming here to live with me? Well, I just couldn't be any more excited than I already was.

"Yes, I want you to live with me!" I exclaimed and he swept me up in his arms one more time, just like yesterday.

"Then, this is the first time that I'm going to put a diaper on you."

JOHN'S EPILOGUE

So, there she was, lying in the bed. I had the diaper, which I was now holding in my hand. "Come on, scoot over. Give me some space," I ordered and she obeyed, showing me that there was a good sign that our life together might happen smoothly, without anything getting in the way.

Not to mention that Lindsey looked so cute, so even the thought of punishing her one day wasn't something that I wanted to consider right now.

I laid the diaper down on the bed and then she came over, settling her butt on the soft material. "Wow, it's so comfy, Daddy," she said, smiling and showing me how pretty her teeth were. Well, it couldn't be any different. I was planning on making Lindsey follow so many rules. One of them would be that she couldn't spend her days without brushing her teeth after eating anything. She wasn't going to like it, but it wasn't like she was going to have much say in it.

"As it should be, for someone as cute as you are," I said after pulling the sides of the diaper and then securing it around her. When it was tight and secure around her after applying all the necessary creams and even the talcum, I lied down on the bed, putting my arm around her. I just needed to feel her body. I needed to feel how warm and inviting she was.

And even now, seeing her face, I kissed her one more time. "I love you so much. I want you to know that."

"But I already know that. You don't need to say it again, even though I like to hear that coming from you, so it's not like I'm complaining."

I moved my hand over her leg. Then, I found her pacifier sitting on top of the nightstand and snatched it. I showed it to her and she opened her lips. Lindsey was always so submissive and acceptive of everything I wanted to do with her. So, thinking that, I put the pacifier between her lips and she closed them around it, accepting it.

I flicked my finger on her nose. "Now that you have my pacifier in your mouth, you can't say anything. I forbid you from saying anything. You are to remain with your lips sealed while I pamper you with love," I said, sneaking my hand under her diaper and finding her clit, rubbing it and shooting ripples of pleasure in her body. She loved it. I could see it in the way that she closed her eyes, started to moan and groan, and especially after her body started to tremble, showing me that she had just orgasmed.

"Oh Daddy, that was so good," she said even while she had the pacifier in her mouth. Well, I couldn't just have that without doing something about it. I was going to have to discipline her for the infraction she committed, and I was sure that, despite all the things going on in her mind, she was going to enjoy it, no matter how painful it was going to be.

"You are my everything."

LINDSEY'S EPILOGUE

So, I was his everything. In other circumstances, I would've thought something like this would never happen, but now it was part of my being. We were somewhere else. We were with someone else. His name was Paul and he was a doctor. He was taller than me like pretty much everyone was. He had short, dark hair, dark eyes, a stubble on his face, and he was stunning, though of course not as stunning as John was.

Given that he had just arrived in town, we were helping him set up his things in his new house. It was a big house, so there was space here for someone else. Was he looking for a partner? I didn't know. We hadn't asked him anything about that.

"No, but I really don't think that I'm going to find the love of my life here anyway," he said when he was coming inside the house with his arms holding a huge box with his things.

He knew about me and my Little side. Now that I was already living with John for some months, there were times when I felt comfortable sharing with other people about this side of me, so this was one of those moments. Not to mention that, outside, it was dark, so it wasn't like anybody was going to see me wearing only my diaper and my onesie and bra. I had a sippy cup with orange juice in my right hand, from which I took occasional sips. It was over-the-top tasty.

I was sitting on the couch's right arm, which they had already finished putting in the living room.

"You never know what might happen in the future. You might

find the person you want to be with."

That was John who said that. He also had a box in his arms, which he carried inside the house. He put it down in the room. It probably contained some things that Paul was going to put in the TV rack.

"I'm not so hopeful about that, though knowing that someone like Lindsey lives here, I am beginning to feel I might be wrong about it."

He said that after putting down the box he was carrying. He started to open it while looking at me with curious eyes. What did he mean by 'someone more like me?' I asked myself, wondering if perhaps he was a Daddy.

After all these things that happened in my life, I wouldn't be surprised.

The End

Don't forget to check the next page for a sneak peek to 'SEAL's Desperate Little' and other stories by me. You can also leave your review. It really helps me!

TEASER: SEAL'S DESPERATE LITTLE

Duty Calls - 2

The sun, so hot and so bright in the sky, shining light on my face. I hid it with my arm, making my way to my car. It was parked in front of the café where I worked. Around me, not many people perambulating on the streets. Only a couple of stragglers here and there.

I reached my car and opened the door. After sitting down, I already felt a lot more comfortable and better about everything. Even though I kind of liked working in that café, it wasn't for me and I didn't think it would ever be. I wished to be doing something different with my life.

Something more grandiose, maybe traveling around the world, meeting new people, new cultures, and doing all that with someone important to me. Someone that I could call my love.

I shook my head, closing my eyes tightly.

I doubted that any of those things would happen. I was stuck here in Sudbury. The town was nice, but it was too small. More and more, that was what I always thought, and I couldn't change it.

One of the reasons why I thought my life would always remain this way was because I was a Little. Always had been. Ever since I was just a teen, when I was still a child, I always saw myself with different eyes. I had always liked to play with my toys, always liked to watch cartoons, and be someone else from who society wanted me to be.

I took a deep breath and reopened my eyes. At least, here I had a house. It wasn't big and it certainly would never impress anyone, but it was my place. The good thing about living in Sudbury was that saving up money was easy, even though I didn't make much.

My expenses here were minimal. The house itself had been a gift from my late parents. They passed away a long time ago. I was still a young teen when it happened. When they died, my aunt took care of me, and she was the most important person in the world to me.

She was so important that I always told her everything about my life, including the fact that the house now had a playroom with a huge crib in it. Most people, upon finding out about that, would have stopped talking to me and maybe even called the police on me, but not her. She was different. She was more willing to accept things that challenged her understanding of the world.

I turned the key in the ignition, thinking that the engine of the car was going to turn on, but it didn't. It made a sound that suggested it was dead, but it didn't make me feel scared that the engine wasn't going to work. In fact, this was far from the first time something like this was happening. There had been so many times when the engine died on me, and I knew I just needed to turn the key one more time so that it finally worked.

And that I did, hoping that it was going to achieve the result I wanted, but then I was disappointed when it didn't. I squinted my eyes slowly, looking at the console and finding out that nothing appeared to be wrong with any part of the car, including the engine. If something was wrong with it, it would be showing me so right now.

"What the hell's going on with you?" I asked, shaking my head in disbelief. I couldn't believe that I was going to have to step out of the car and pop open the engine compartment.

No pointing in delaying it, I thought after opening the door and then going to the front of the car. Just when I was going to pop open the lid, I noticed footsteps approaching me.

Then, I turned around and found someone that made my body feel hot all over, and I didn't know why. Or maybe I did and I didn't want to admit it to myself.

The man was hot. He was stunning, jaw-dropping, and that was putting it mildly. I just didn't think that someone like him was living here in Sudbury. Where had he been all this time? I asked myself, realizing that I was pushing my body against the frame of the car.

Why was I feeling so submissive and small in his presence?

Again, the reason for that was typical. Just like so many other men I had seen in my life, both here in Sudbury and on TV, I was beginning to develop a crush on him.

Of course that was what I was going to be feeling. It wasn't just the fact that he was stunning and so tall, but also that his body was… Well, suffice to say that it made me want to see him naked. I couldn't help but wonder what he was like without his clothes on.

But I knew that would never happen, so I was smashing my hopes right at this moment. No point in building false hope, especially when there was a good chance that he wasn't even coming in my direction. Maybe he was just going to walk past me, and if that happened, it wouldn't be a surprise.

After all, why would anyone – and especially someone of his caliber – even look twice at me?

But that was the thing. Whoever he was, he was staring right at me, and that was only making my body feel hotter. I felt like I was running a fever, and I was certain that he was thinking I looked funny. If that was the case, I wouldn't blame him.

I just hoped that I was going to stop whatever was happening here before I made a fool of myself.

He stopped when he was no more than a couple of feet from me. I could see it in his face and eyes. He wasn't someone that had never left Sudbury. He had gone elsewhere, perhaps even out of the country. He had this vibe around him that he had seen things he didn't want to share with anyone. Some scars painted his face, and even though he was Caucasian like I was, his skin had faint but visible signs that he had been under the sun for years in a faraway country.

SIMILAR BOOKS

SERIES - MAFIA CUPIDS

A mafia setting with generous amounts of plus size dynamics.

1. His Plus Size Little
2. Hitman's Plus Size Little
3. Biker's Plus Size Little

SERIES - BIG ME

MM ABDL. Lots of age play, sweetness, peppered with steamy scenes, and sprinkled with age gap dynamics.

1. Pampering Little Miguel
2. Endless Crayons
3. Teaching Little Jerry

Or download all of these books in this bundle:

Sweet Holidays

ABOUT THE AUTHOR

Amanda King writes sweet ABDL, age play romances. Packaged with steamy scenes, her books are fast-paced and, more often than not, they deeply explore the world of age gap relationships.

When she isn't writing, she's reading for inspiration. Some of her most popular stories are "Pampering Little Miguel" and "Endless Crayons."